King Midas and the Golden Touch

Retold by Jenny Giles

Illustrated by Loma Tilders

NELSON PRICE MILBURN

Once upon a time,
there was a wealthy king called Midas.
He lived with his wife and daughter
in a grand palace.

All around the palace
there were beautiful gardens
with a clear stream flowing through them.
King Midas had all he could wish for,
and he loved his family
more than anything else
in the world...

except for gold.

2

3

Every morning, King Midas would go
down the stairs that led
to his great treasure room.
There he would count his bars of gold
and gaze at all his shining coins.

But as time went by,
gold became much more important
than his family to King Midas.
One day, when his daughter brought him
marigolds from the garden,
he just threw them away.
"These flowers are not made of gold," he said.
"Only real gold can make me happy."

5

One morning, King Midas looked around
his treasure room.
"I will **never** have all the gold that I want,"
he said to himself.
"How I wish that everything I touched
would turn to gold.
Then I would be truly happy."

Just as King Midas finished speaking,
a strange figure appeared.
"Your wish can come true, Midas,"
he said, "for I can give you
the gift of the Golden Touch.
From now on, everything you touch
will turn to gold."

King Midas was delighted.
He looked down at his clothes
and saw that they were golden.

He went out of his treasure room
and locked the door behind him.
The door, the key and the handle
became golden also.

King Midas rushed out into the gardens.
There he watched the flowers and trees
turning to gold at his lightest touch.
"Oh!" he cried.
"I am the richest man in the world.
How happy I am!"

King Midas went into the palace
to have his breakfast.
As he sat down, his chair turned to gold.
So did his knife and fork and plate.
But when he began to eat,
he found that the food
was hard and golden.
He couldn't bite it
or swallow it!

At that moment, King Midas realised
that he had asked for too much.
His eyes filled with tears.

His daughter saw that he was sad,
and she ran to put her arms around him.

King Midas saw
what was going to happen.
He moved back, but he was too late.
His daughter touched him, and at once
she turned into a golden statue.

"What have I done?" cried King Midas.
"My beautiful daughter is now lifeless!
Oh, how I wish that I had **never**
asked for the Golden Touch."

Just then, the strange figure
appeared again.
"Have you learned your lesson, Midas?"
he asked.
"Do you know that gold alone
cannot make you happy?"

"Yes! Yes!" replied King Midas.
"Please give me back my daughter!
She is dearer to me than all the gold
in the world."

"Do as I say, and the Golden Touch shall be taken from you," said the figure.
"You must go and bathe in the stream which flows through your gardens.
When the water washes over you, the things that you touched will no longer be made of gold."

"Oh, thank you!" cried King Midas, and he ran down to the stream.

As he bathed, the gold fell from his clothes and became sparkling sand beneath his feet.

King Midas looked around him.
All the flowers were brightly coloured.
All the leaves were green again.

Then, to his great joy,
he saw his daughter running towards him.

And as he walked with his family
through the palace gardens,
King Midas was truly happy, at last.